For Amelie Traynor and Sophia Kennedy – I.W.

For Catherine and Martin – R.R.

First published 2010 by Macmillan Children's Books
a division of Macmillan Publishers Limited
20 New Wharf Road, London N1 9RR
Basingstoke and Oxford
Associated companies throughout the world
www.panmacmillan.com

ISBN: 978-0-230-71224-9 (HB)
ISBN: 978-0-330-50956-5 (PB)

Text copyright © Ian Whybrow 2010
Illustrations copyright © Rosie Reeve 2010
Moral rights asserted.

1 3 5 7 9 8 6 4 2

A CIP catalogue record for this book
is available from the British Library.

Printed in Italy

Bella Goes to School

Ian Whybrow

Illustrated by Rosie Reeve

MACMILLAN CHILDREN'S BOOKS

Bella was putting her bowl into the dishwasher
when her big brother Ben came rushing downstairs.

"What's the hurry, Big Brother Rushabout?" said Mummy Rabbit.
"I need my gym kit!" said Ben. "Quick, Mum! Please!"
"Look in your drawer," said Mummy Rabbit.
"Then come and eat your porridge."

"I'm no good at gym," mumbled Bella.
"Will I have to do gym when I start school?"
Mummy Rabbit didn't hear her.

"Are you ready to go, Sophie?" Mummy said.
"Daddy has to leave in ten minutes."

"I'm just finishing my story," said Sophie.
"It's in my best writing."
"Well done, Big Sister Tidypaws," said Daddy Rabbit.
"Now, run and brush your teeth."

"I can't do writing," sighed Bella.
"Will I get into trouble when I go to school?"

"Don't be such a worrier, Bella," said Mummy Rabbit.
"You'll have lots of fun at school. And you're a
good learner. You'll love it once you get started."

Bella waved goodbye to her big brother and sister.
Then she got dressed all by herself.

"That's my big girl!" said Mummy Rabbit.
"But I can't tie my shoelaces," groaned Bella.
"Yes you can, if you keep trying," said Mummy Rabbit.
"Try it like this."

Bella tried.

No good.

She tried again.

"I nearly did it that time!" Bella laughed.
"I told you you were a good learner!" said Mummy Rabbit.

Later that morning, Mummy Rabbit heard
Bella playing at being Teacher.

"**Bad dolly!**" she shouted.
"You stand in the corner!"

"**Bad bear!**" she shouted. "I said
no talking! And Monkey, this writing
is silly and scribbly," said Bella.
"You are a bad learner! Do it all again!"

"Oh dear, Bella," said Mummy Rabbit.
"It's much more fun than that at school.
And I'm sure the teacher won't shout
at you. Why don't I call Joel's house
and see if he can come
round to play?"

Joel brought his ball with him.

"Catch!" he called.

Bella dropped it and made a face.

"Put out your arms like this," said Joel, and threw it again.
This time Bella caught it, no trouble at all.

"Well done, Bella!" said Joel.

"Now I'll teach you cartwheels," said Bella.
Joel tried but he couldn't get the trick right away.

"Keep trying," said Bella.
So he tried again, but he still couldn't do a cartwheel.

"Never mind, we can try that again later," Bella said.
"Let me show you something else."

So she showed him how to do a backward roll,
and Joel did it even better than she did!

"Drinks for the gym stars," said Mummy Rabbit.
"We're not gym stars!" laughed Bella.

"Well, that looked like pretty good gym to me,"
said Mummy Rabbit. "What good learners!"

So Bella and Joel drank their drinks
and then they showed Mummy Rabbit . . .

headstands,

handstands,

splits,

and star jumps.

After that, they watched Junior Bunny Hour on TV.
First there was counting, and then the alphabet.
"There's a J for Joel!" said Joel.
"And a B for Bella!" said Bella. "I know, let's
do our letters and numbers!"

So they ran out into the garden.

First they practised their counting. One carrot, two carrots . . . all the way up to ten.

Then they did their letters. There was a J for Joel, and a B for Bella.

"My goodness!" said the lady next door. "What lovely writing!
You two are so clever. I didn't know you went to school!"
"We don't yet, but we're starting soon," said Joel.

"And we can do catching and gym already,
not just letters," explained Bella. "Look!"
And they showed her some very fast skipping.

"We can count too, but we can't
do sums actually," puffed Joel.
"No, but our teacher will teach us sums at
school and we're good learners." said Bella.
"Look!" She bent down and . . . guess what?

She tied up her shoelace, all by herself!

When the day came to start school, Bella
was too excited to wait for Ben and Sophie.

Joel came to fetch her and they scooted together all the way to their new class.

It wasn't long
before they made
lots of new friends,

and did all sorts
of exciting new things.

And Bella found out that
Mummy Rabbit was right after all . . .

. . . school was lots of fun!